Jojo and the...

...Food Fight!

WRITTEN BY Didier Lévy

ILLUSTRATED BY Nathalie Dieterlé

TRANSLATED BY Lisa Rosinsky

Barefoot Books
step inside a story

For many days and many nights . . .

. . . there was a **food fight frenzy** in the jungle!
All the animals were angry with each other.
Insults and rotten fruit flew
in every direction.

Suddenly, a little elephant with a pink parasol
walked right into the middle of the battlefield.

"Hello, I seem to have lost my memory,"
he said, looking all around. "Has anyone seen it?
I'm sure I left it here somewhere."

The animals turned and stared at him. For just a moment, they stopped fighting and throwing fruit. **"Jojo!"** cried the lion. "Move out of the way! You're going to get hit!"

The little elephant lifted his head. "Is that me? Jojo? That's my name? Do we know each other?"

"Come on, Jojo," said the lion. "You know perfectly well that we live next door to each other!"

"Oh, really?" said the elephant. "I don't remember you. I've lost my memory!"

Jojo poked his pink parasol at a banana that had landed on the ground.

"And what on earth is this silly-looking thing?"

The monkey's eyes snapped open wide.
"You don't remember what a banana is?"

"No . . . you'll have to remind me." Jojo shook
his head sadly. "*Ba-NA-na*? That's what you call it?"

The lion and the monkey
waved white flags
and shouted,

"TIME OUT!

Five-minute
cease-fire!

We have to
HELP JOJO!"

They walked up to Jojo.

"Are you going to help me find my memory?"
asked the little elephant.

The monkey took the banana, peeled it and held it out to Jojo.
"Taste it!"

"Oh!" said Jojo. "You're supposed to eat this funny thing?"

Then the crocodile came over and planted Jojo's pink parasol
in the ground to make a table.

Jojo sat down at the parasol table and took a bite of the banana.

"Mmm," he said with a big smile.
"Delicious. May I have another one?"

The lion roared,

"WHO HAS ANOTHER BANANA FOR JOJO?"

Within moments, all the animals came out of their hiding places, waving ripe yellow bananas.

"Oh, how nice!" cried Jojo. "Is it snack time? I love snack time!"

The animals sat down around the parasol table, glaring at each other suspiciously.

"Are any of these other animals
our friends, too?" Jojo asked the lion.

"Of course, we're all friends," the animals said. "We go to school together!"

Jojo tilted his head, looking confused.

"And do you always fight like this at school, too?"

The animals looked at each other for a moment.

Then the monkey said, "Well, no."

"We all used to be friends," said the hippopotamus.

"But then **what happened**?" asked Jojo.

All the animals pointed at each other.

"He started it!"

"No, she did!"

"He hit me first —"

"She called me names —"

They were all about to start throwing fruit again
when Jojo tapped the table.

"Excuse me! We called time out, didn't we?
And when someone calls time out, that means TIME OUT."

Everyone froze.

Then, the animals peeled their bananas. And since they were very delicious bananas, much better for eating than for throwing at each other, everyone began to relax and smile.

"I have some mangoes, too," said the kangaroo. "Anyone want one?" She took a few plump mangoes out of her pouch.

"I could share some papayas," said the lion.

Before you could blink, star fruits, passion fruits, pomegranates and plums had appeared as if by magic.

What a feast! Everyone ate as much fruit
as they wanted, and a good mood spread over the table.

As they ate, the animals began to remember all the good times
they'd had together, not so very long ago.

Jojo smiled. "Isn't this nice? It reminds me of my birthday
party last year, when you all came over to my house.
Remember?"

Everyone fell silent.

"WE THOUGHT YOU LOST YOUR MEMORY?!"

the animals cried.

"I guess I just found it!" replied Jojo, with a mischievous grin.

"You tricked us!" the animals shouted.

But they were laughing now, not angry.

They all threw their banana peels at Jojo, who was laughing, too.

And for the rest of the day,
all the animals celebrated.

Late into the night, even after the moon rose high in the sky,
they danced and played together.

For peace and friendship
had returned to the jungle.

THE END

Barefoot Books
2067 Massachusetts Ave
Cambridge, MA 02140

Barefoot Books
29/30 Fitzroy Square
London, W1T 6LQ

Graphic design by Sarah Soldano, Barefoot Books
English-language edition edited by Lisa Rosinsky, Barefoot Books
Reproduction by Bright Arts, Hong Kong
Printed in China on 100% acid-free paper
This book was typeset in Might Could Pencil and Mr Lucky
The illustrations were prepared in colored ink and colored pencils

ISBN 978-1-78285-732-7

British Cataloguing-in-Publication Data:
a catalogue record for this book is available from the British Library
Library of Congress Cataloging-in-Publication Data
is available upon request

7 9 8 6